Story by Paul Shipton
Pictures by Beccy Blake

dingles&company

Summer vacation was approaching and Roz wanted to do something special.

"Perhaps you could join a soccer team?" said Dad.

"Or take dance lessons?" suggested Mom.

"No thanks," said Roz. "I want to go to Clown School."

Mom and Dad read the leaflet about the summer school.

"It looks like **lots** of fun!" said Roz as persuasively as she could.

Mom and Dad talked it over.

"Well . . . OK," they said at last.

Roz jumped up and punched the air.

"**YES!**"

PLEASE!

2

Clown School started the next week.

Roz was excited as she marched into the room. The other people all looked much older, but she didn't mind. She hurried to a table at the front and sat there eagerly waiting for the first lesson to begin.

The door opened and a tall clown came into the room.

"My name is Mr. Bozo," he announced in a deep, serious voice. "I will be your teacher."

A big smile was painted on the teacher's face, but under it his mouth was grim and as straight as an iron rod.

"Learning to be a clown is not all fun and games," he said. "I expect you all to work very hard and study a lot."

"Oh dear," thought Roz nervously. "This isn't what I expected. I'm here to have **fun**!"

In the first lesson, Mr. Bozo handed out red noses to everyone in the class.

"A clown is not a proper clown without a red nose," he declared. "Put this on and do not lose it!"

Roz put on her red nose, but it felt tight. Very tight . . .

It stayed on for about two seconds before popping off.

It shot forward and hit Mr. Bozo in the eye.

"That's **not funny**," growled the teacher.

In the following lesson, Mr. Bozo showed them the rest of the clown costume.

"A proper clown must wear baggy pants and big, flat shoes," he explained.

Roz put her hand up. "Why?"

"Because they are **funny**," replied Mr. Bozo as if he was explaining that two plus two equals four.

The rest of the class looked at the clown costume, but nobody laughed.

The class had to try walking in clown shoes. It was difficult to balance and a lot of the class wobbled, but only one of them couldn't do it at all. Only one tripped and bumped into the teacher.

"Sorry!" said Roz.

"**Not funny** at all," snapped Mr. Bozo.

"So how was Clown School?" Roz's mom asked when she picked her up. "Lots of fun?"

"It was pretty good," mumbled Roz.

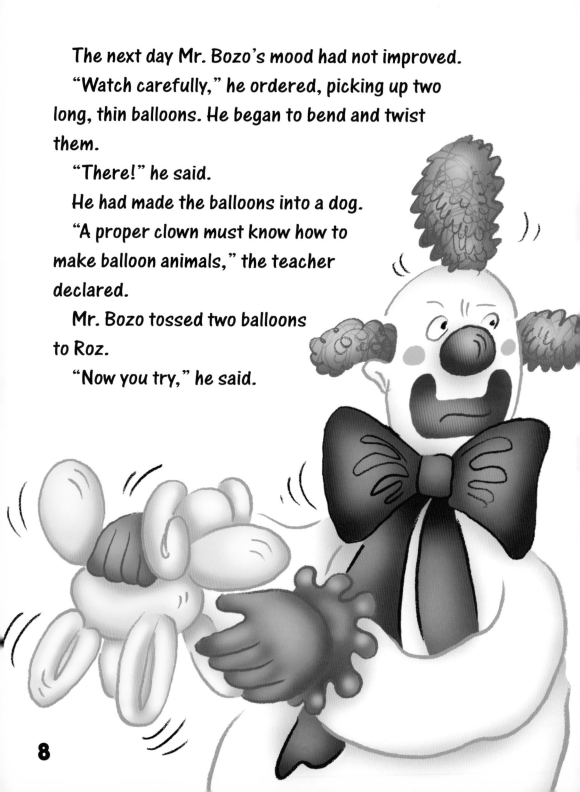

The next day Mr. Bozo's mood had not improved.

"Watch carefully," he ordered, picking up two long, thin balloons. He began to bend and twist them.

"There!" he said.

He had made the balloons into a dog.

"A proper clown must know how to make balloon animals," the teacher declared.

Mr. Bozo tossed two balloons to Roz.

"Now you try," he said.

The balloons squeaked in the silence of the classroom as Roz tried to bend and twist them.

At last she made . . . a big mess!

A big mess

"Try again." Mr. Bozo sighed. This time the balloons came undone in Roz's hands.

Finally she just held up one of the straight balloons and said, "There! It's a snake having a stretch!"

"That isn't the **least bit** funny," snarled Mr. Bozo.

"How was school today?" Dad asked as Roz clambered into the car at the end of the second day. "Still having fun?"

"Sort of," said Roz quietly. She didn't want to admit it, but she was starting to think that Clown School had been a big mistake.

The next morning, Mr. Bozo rode into class on a bike. A tiny bike.

"All proper clowns can ride these little bikes," he announced.

The clowns practiced riding on the little bikes. Most of them got the hang of it.

Not Roz!

"Sorry!" she said when she fell off for the fifth time.

"Sorry!" she cried when she ran over the teacher's foot for the tenth time.

OW!

custard pies

"That is not even a **tiny bit** funny!" grumbled Mr. Bozo.

In the next lesson, Mr. Bozo pointed to a flower in the buttonhole of his jacket.

"See this lovely flower?" he said to a clown in the front row. "Come and smell it." When the clown leaned forward cautiously to sniff it, Mr. Bozo squirted him in the face with a jet of water.

SPLAT!

"All proper clowns can do tricks like that," he explained.

He told Roz to come and smell the flower. She started toward the front of the class but she still wasn't very good at walking in those big clown shoes. She tripped and stumbled into Mr. Bozo. The water from the trick flower shot out . . .
into Mr. Bozo's face.

"That is not even **a teensy bit** funny!" he yelled, as the painted clown smile slid down his wet face. The expression it left behind was not a happy one.

Mr. Bozo had calmed down by the start of the next lesson. He stood at the front of the class with a custard pie in the palm of his hand.

"Every proper clown knows how to throw a custard pie perfectly," he informed the class.

He asked two clowns to come to the front. The teacher handed the pie to one of them and began to explain how to throw it. It was a long, complicated explanation.

40°

splat area

custard pies

14

After five minutes of this detailed explanation, Roz found it hard to pay attention. She gazed out of the window. She looked at the park, wishing she could be playing there instead of being stuck in the classroom.

She spotted a duck swimming in the pond.

"Duck!" she said aloud.

One of the two clowns at the front thought that Roz was talking to her. So she ducked.

The pie sailed over the clown who had ducked.
Instead, it hit Mr. Bozo.

SPLAT!

It was a great shot – right in the face.

"Sorry!" said Roz.

Under the thick layer of
custard pie, all that could be seen
were Mr. Bozo's eyes flashing
and his mouth roaring.

"**Not funny!**" he shouted.
"**Not a teensy, tiny bit
funny** at all!"

At lunchtime Roz sat on a bench in the park all by herself.

"I'm no good at clown tricks," she thought glumly.

She was so lost in her thoughts that she didn't even notice the big man running through the park with a heavy bag slung over his shoulder.

The man didn't see Roz's enormous clown shoes sticking out across the footpath. He tripped over them.

Sorry!

Roz leaped up to help the man. The sudden movement made her red nose pop off again.

It hit the man in the left eye.

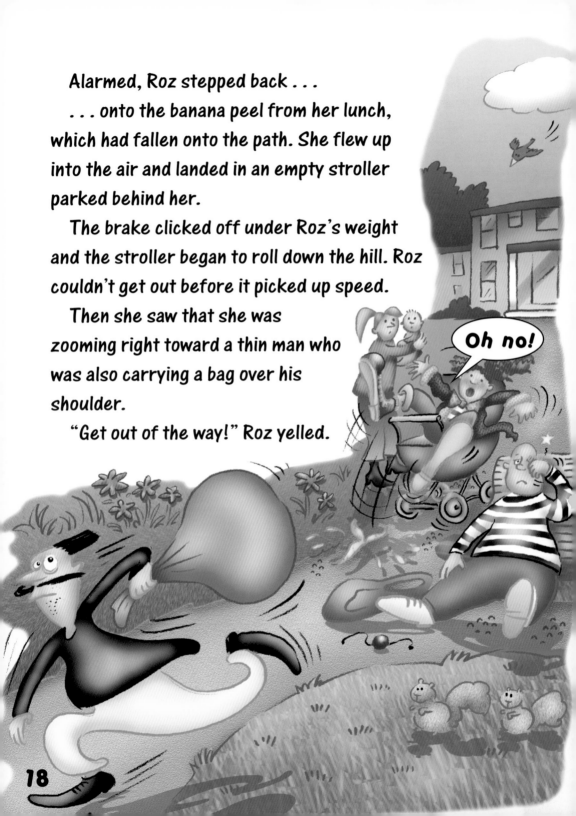

Alarmed, Roz stepped back . . .

. . . onto the banana peel from her lunch, which had fallen onto the path. She flew up into the air and landed in an empty stroller parked behind her.

The brake clicked off under Roz's weight and the stroller began to roll down the hill. Roz couldn't get out before it picked up speed.

Then she saw that she was zooming right toward a thin man who was also carrying a bag over his shoulder.

"Get out of the way!" Roz yelled.

Oh no!

The man whirled around just in time to see a runaway stroller hurtling toward him. But he didn't have time to jump out of the way. He tumbled back into the stroller as it struck him. On down the hill zoomed the runaway stroller.

"Sorry!" shouted Roz to the man. She was scared now because she could no longer see where they were going.

"Help!" shouted the man. He was scared because he **could** see where they were going – straight toward the bakery at the bottom of the hill!

A woman from the bakery was carrying a large batch of custard pies into the shop. She dropped the tray when she heard the speeding stroller bump into the curb.

Roz tumbled forward onto the pavement, but the man in the stroller flew into the air.

SPLAT!

He landed headfirst in the custard pies.

The skinny man hopped up and quickly grabbed his bag. He tried to run away, but the ground was too slippery now, with so much custard all over it.

Before the man could get up, a police officer ran up.

"I can explain everything," began Roz.

But the police officer just grabbed the man and snapped a pair of handcuffs on him.

"Got you!" she said with a grin.

The police officer turned to Roz. "Well done!" she said. "You've helped us catch Slippery Sid. He's just robbed the bank on High Street."

"What?" Only now did Roz notice that the man's bag was stuffed full of money.

A police officer marched down the hill. He was leading the other man, who had tripped over Roz's shoes.

"Look! She helped us catch Bad Burt, too," said the police officer. "She's a real hero!"

The police officers led the two miserable bank robbers to a waiting police car.

Roz was so stunned that it took her a few moments to realize that someone else was standing behind her. It was Mr. Bozo!

"I was in the park and I saw everything," he said. "You did all of the clown tricks very well. Perhaps one day you **could** be a proper clown, after all."

"Thanks, but I'm not sure I **want** to be a clown," answered Roz. "Perhaps I'll be a police officer when I grow up."

Mr. Bozo sighed and turned to go back to the school.

"Wait, Mr. Bozo!" shouted Roz. "Duck!"

The teacher gave a quick glance at the duck in the pond.

"Yes, I can see the duck," he said impatiently. "I am not interested in ducks. Ducks are not funny at all."

SPLAT!

The custard pie hit him in the face!

"I **did** tell you to duck!" Roz laughed. "You have to admit that it was just a little bit funny."

Against his will, Mr. Bozo's mouth curled up at the corners in the beginnings of a real smile. The smile grew and then he, too, began to laugh.